I'm a Big Brother

This book is dedicated to every little boy who has just become a big brother.

Mommy and Daddy were gone for a while
Then they came back home with a great big smile

Wrapped up in a blanket held by my mother
Was my brand new, tiny, baby brother!

Daddy showed me baby's bib

His clothes, his toys and baby's crib

And tiny hats for baby's head

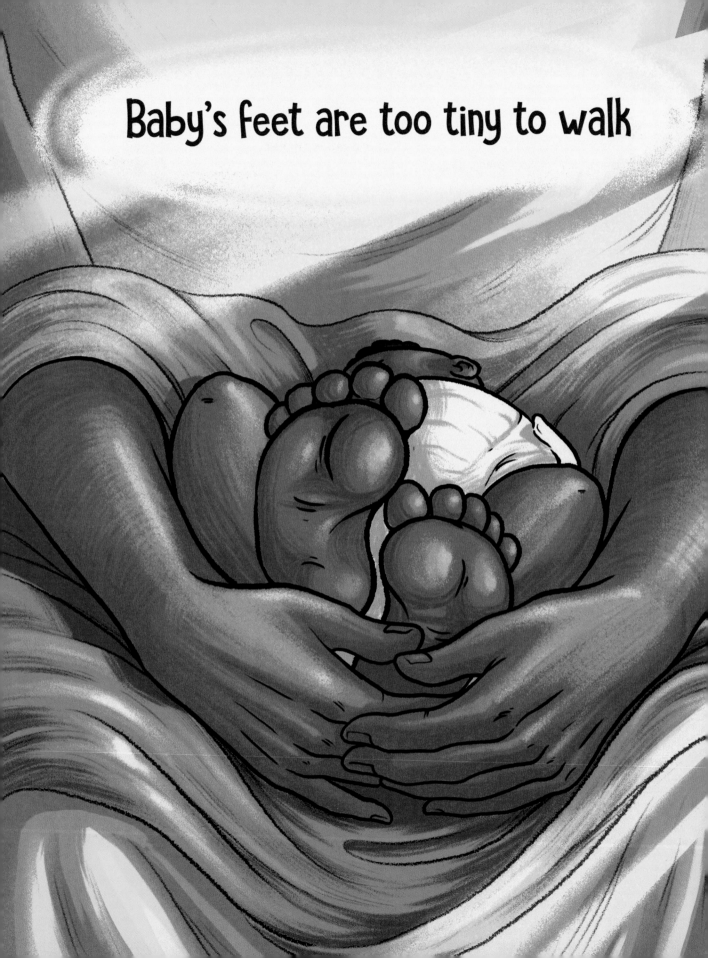

Baby's feet are too tiny to walk

And baby doesn't know how to talk

But if baby feels like something's wrong
His cry is loud and long and strong!

Baby is short and I am tall

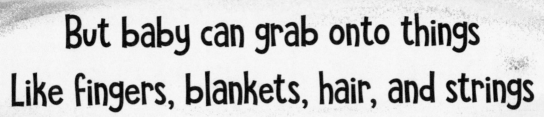

But baby can grab onto things
Like fingers, blankets, hair, and strings

Baby loves baths in his tiny tub

I play with my duck
And sing Rub-a-dub-dub

Mommy told me she can see
What a good brother I will be

After she kisses me goodnight,
mom tucks me in to bed real tight

I'm so glad baby is here
I'll be big brother of the year

Even though life with a baby is new
I love being a big brother and so will you!